wet

For my parents,
Tim and Laura

Henry Holt and Company
Publishers since 1866
175 Fifth Avenue
New York, New York 10010
mackids.com

Library of Congress Cataloging-in-Publication Data is available.
ISBN 978-1-62779-775-7

Our books may be purchased in bulk for promotional, educational, or business use. Please contact your
local bookseller or the Macmillan Corporate and Premium Sales Department at (800) 221-7945 ext. 5442
or by e-mail at MacmillanSpecialMarkets@macmillan.com.

First Edition—2017
Printed in China by RR Donnelley Asia Printing Solutions Ltd., Dongguan City, Guangdong Province

1   3   5   7   9   10   8   6   4   2

wet

Carey Sookocheff

GODWIN BOOKS
Henry Holt and Company • New York

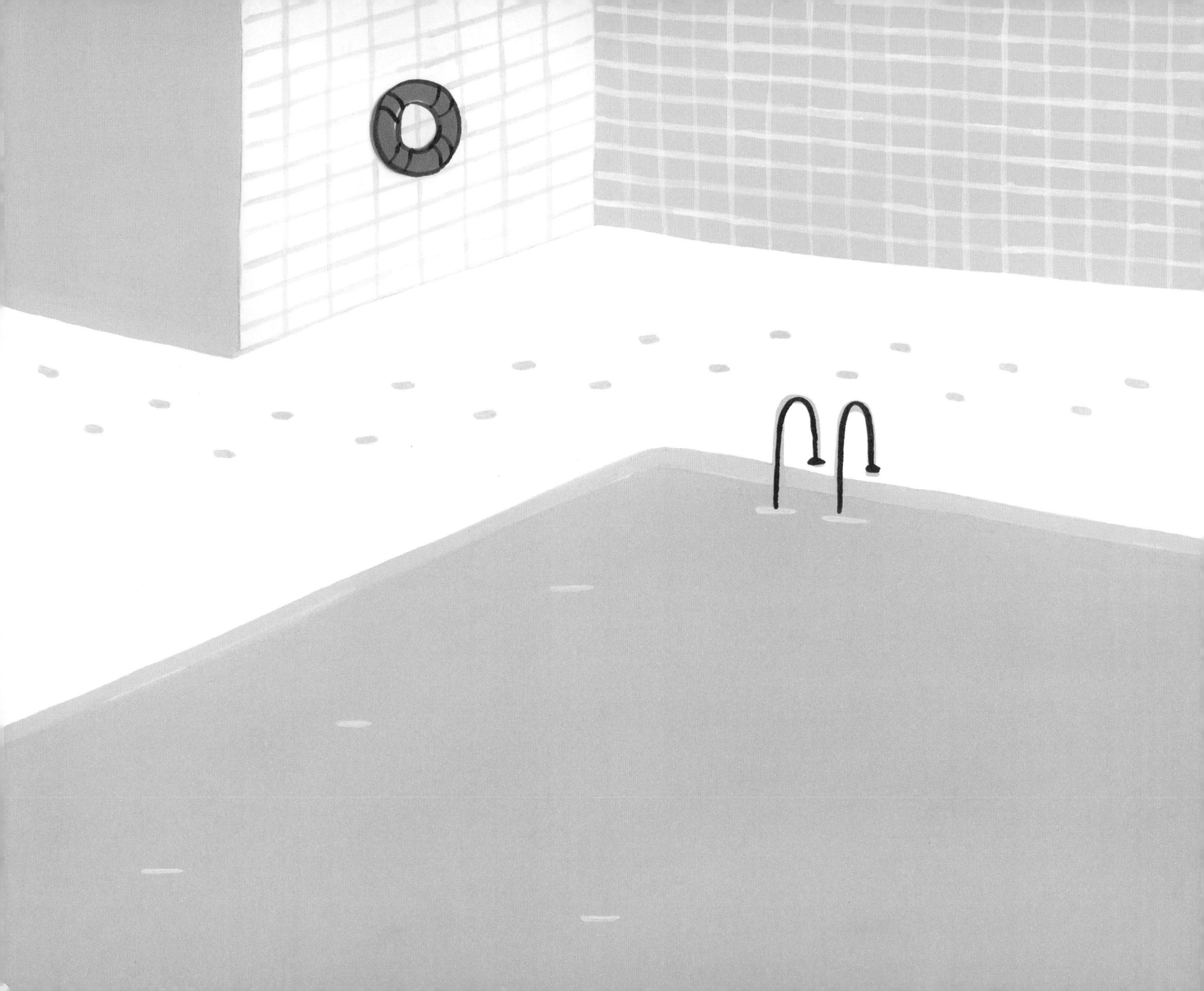

At the pool my feet get wet first.

Sometimes

I get wet

VERY

slowly.

Sometimes I get wet quickly,

and my friends get wet, too.

We like getting all-the-way wet,

but some people just get halfway wet.

Everything gets wet in the rain,

but some people just get halfway wet.

Everything gets wet in the rain,

except my cat.

My fish is always wet.

So is the floor at school . . .

. . . and the bottom of the slide.

Last week the park bench was wet, too.

My hands get wet when I wash them,

and my shirt gets wet when I dry them.

My dog's water bowl is wet.

So is her tongue and my socks.

Sometimes it's fun to get wet,

and sometimes it's not.

My face gets wet when I cry.

So does my dad's shoulder.

After getting wet and dirty,

I have to get wet again.

And so do my clothes.

At the end of the day

nothing is wet...

. . . except my face, from good-night kisses.